For Reg and Muriel ~ E B

Here's hoping we all find our own pot of gold ~ C P

Copyright © 2008 by Good Books, Intercourse, PA 17534
International Standard Book Number: 978-1-56148-617-5

Library of Congress Catalog Card Number: 2007032367

Text copyright © Elizabeth Baguley 2008
Illustrations copyright © Caroline Pedler 2008

Original edition published in English by Little Tiger Press, an imprint of
Magi Publications, London, England, 2008.

Printed in China

Library of Congress Cataloging-in-Publication Data

Baguley, Elizabeth.
Little Pip and the rainbow wish / Elizabeth Baguley ;
illustrated by Caroline Pedler.
p. cm.
Summary: Pip, a shy little mouse, decides to catch a rainbow to give to
Spike and Milly so that they will be his friends.
ISBN 978-1-56148-617-5 (hardcover)
[1. Friendship--Fiction. 2. Rainbow--Fiction. 3. Bashfulness--Fiction.
4. Mice--Fiction.] I. Pedler, Caroline, ill. II. Title.

PZ7.B1422Lhp 2008

[E]--dc22

2007032367

Little Pip and the
Rainbow Wish

Elizabeth Baguley   Caroline Pedler

Good Books

Intercourse, PA 17534
800/762-7171
www.GoodBooks.com

Hidden away, small and wet, Pip huddled beneath a hedge. While out in the open, Milly and Spike played puddle-splashing and dodge-the-raindrop.

Pip wanted to join in, but he was such a shy little mouse that he couldn't think of a way to ask.

Pip watched as Spike gave
Milly a dandelion seed head.
Together they wiggled and
whooped around it. Perhaps,
Pip thought, if I had
something to give them,
they would play with *me*.
He looked around but could
see only scratchy stones
and patchy sky.

Just at that moment . . .

. . . a shining rainbow lit up the clouds.
What a present *that* would be for Milly and
Spike! They could slide down it, balance on
it, make a tent under its colors. And he
would be their friend.

But the rainbow was so far away . . .

. . . too high to reach on
the tips of his paws . . .

too far away to catch
with a bendy stick . . .

and his bounce was
just not bouncy enough.

No matter what he tried,
the rainbow was very, very up
and Pip was very, very down.

"What are you doing?" asked Milly,
who had stopped playing to watch.

Pip's tail blushed to its very tip.
"I wanted to catch the . . . er . . . er . . ."
"The rainbow?" said Spike. "That's brilliant! We'll help!"

Spike clambered onto Milly's shoulders. "Come on, Pip," he called. "We need you, too." And he swung Pip right to the top of the mouse-tower.

The tower was sky-high. But then Pip began to wobble . . . the tower began to sway . . .

And
they
all
fell
into
a
jumbly
mouse
heap!

"We could just *wish* for
the rainbow," Pip said,
quietly.

"Good idea!" said Spike,
and together they squeezed
their wish into the sky.

But the rainbow stayed
right where it was.

Then Milly picked up the dandelion seed
head. "Someone could fly to the rainbow!"
she said. "Who's lightest?"

"Me, me!" cried Pip, suddenly not shy at all.

Milly and Spike pulled Pip along, until the
wind scooped him up so high that he could
almost touch the rainbow.

He reached out his
paws. But the seeds
began to fall from the
dandelion, one . . .

by one . . .

by one.

And

Pip

sank

s l o w l y

back

to

earth.

"I didn't catch the rainbow," said Pip, sadly.

"You were very brave," said Milly, hugging him.

"We'll just have to think of another way," said Spike.

But at that very moment, the rain dripped to

a stop and the rainbow melted away and was gone.

"Don't go!" begged Pip. "Please don't go!"

"Don't worry," said Spike. "There'll be another rainbow."

"But I needed it," sniffed Pip, "to give to you and Milly, so that you would be my friends."

"But we *are* your friends!" said Milly.

"Who needs presents anyway?" said Spike.

Then off they raced, all together,
hopping and splashing from puddle
to puddle, until the night sky burst
into a brilliant sparkling of stars.